THE CREATURE IN THE CRYSTAL

BY J. A. DARKE

TEXT BY ERIC STEVENS

ILLUSTRATED BY NEIL EVANS

raintree

a Capstone company — publishers for children

CONTENTS

CHAPTER ONE

The first week of tenth grade was over.

Valarie Stoll would have taken a deep breath and let it out slowly, happy to have that trauma behind her, if the air on the school bus hadn't been so putrid.

Instead, she took a seat near the front but not *too* near the front, put her bag on her lap and closed her eyes. The boy who sat next to her ignored her as he turned half his body back into the aisle and continued his loud conversation with his friend opposite him.

"No, man," the boy said. Val was 92 per cent sure his name was Aiden. Or Eamon.

Maybe Jaden.

"You can't sneak up on him," the boy went on. "If you don't hit him from the front, his shield prevents *all* damage."

Video games, Val thought, seething. It was all anybody talked about. She, though, preferred to fantasize in her own head. For a moment, she recalled her friendship with Ellie Roth down the street.

They were very close – best friends, probably – all through elementary school and some of middle school too. The two girls spent their time together drawing fantastical pictures; writing epic stories; or sometimes just lying together in the grass behind Ellie's house on the corner, staring up at the clouds, and reciting their stories and imaginings aloud.

But then came seventh grade, and when everyone came back from summers away –

at lakes, on family trips, to weeklong music or football or science camps – Ellie was like a totally different person.

"I grew up a lot," she had said with a shrug, flanked by Olive and Mackenzie. She'd grown close to them at a resort in Long Lake, where – just by coincidence – all three girls' families had spent the whole month of July.

"To be honest," Ellie added, glancing quickly at her new friends, "the stuff you and I used to do is sort of embarrassing to me now, you know?"

"Oh," Val had said as her face went red and she wished to be dead. "No, I know. I know what you mean." She forced a laugh. "Me too, obviously."

Olive stared pointedly at Val's T-shirt: an airbrush painting of a unicorn in an enchanted garden. Val had watched the artist make it at a place in the city. Ellie had been there too. She'd even got a T-shirt of her own with elves on it.

"Oh," Val said, looking down at her shoes. "I . . ."

She trailed off, and Olive guffawed. "Don't worry, Valarie," she said. "I'm sure you'll grow up eventually."

With that, the three BFFs had turned and walked away. Val had hardly said two words to Ellie since that first day of seventh grade. In the years since, Val, too, had put away such things as elves and unicorns and magic. But she could never seem to keep up with Ellie in the *cool* department.

Speak of the devil, Val thought as Ellie, Olive and Mackenzie climbed onto the bus, already deep in conversation. They passed her seat without even glancing at her and settled into their usual places at the back.

Val closed her eyes and tried not to hear them, but they were just so *loud*.

"What time should we come over?" That sounded like the voice of a girl who had recently swallowed a chainsaw. Olive.

"Yeah," said another girl, her voice sickly and sweet like the chewing gum she chomped as she spoke. That would be Mackenzie. "I am so excited about this weekend."

At least someone is excited about the holiday weekend, Val thought. There'd be no school on Monday, but instead of doing something, Val would be stuck hosting her cousin Veronica's family, visiting from Chicago.

Her *weird* cousin Veronica. Rather than putting aside fairy stories and fantastic ideas, Ronnie had embraced them with increased enthusiasm. The last time Ronnie came to town, she held a seance at the dining-room table with candles and hand-holding and everything. It was super creepy.

"Um, I'll text you." That was Ellie. Some voices were familiar enough so that even three words and an *um* could make your heart drop into your tummy a little bit. "Like five, probably? Or six? I don't know. My dad will pick up pizzas on his way home from work."

"Work?" Olive said, laughing. "On Saturday?"

"Every Saturday for as long as I can remember," Ellie said.

Val knew that already, obviously. She'd once comforted Ellie because her dad couldn't even be there for Ellie's tenth birthday party.

And now here they were just a few years later and Ellie was having a sleepover without her.

"It doesn't matter," Val mumbled to herself. "I couldn't have gone anyway because I have to hang out with Ronnie all weekend."

"Did you say something to me?" said the boy next to her, glancing over his shoulder at her.

Val smiled awkwardly. "Just talking to myself."

"OK, weirdo," the boy said, and he went back to his conversation about video games.

CHAPTER TWO

The bus drove along Birch Street to the corner of Grove Avenue. Val pushed past the video game boy and hurried off the bus before Ellie could make her way to the front. She was halfway down the street by the time the door closed with a slam and the bus roared around the corner.

Val crossed Dell Avenue and walked quickly past the row of shops on the corner. It sat back from the road, on the far side of a car park.

When she was small, the little row of

shops had done well. It had a good Chinese restaurant, a card and sweet shop and a dry cleaners. In recent years, though, the card shop and Chinese place had closed. Now it was rare to see anyone pull into the car park.

As she passed, Val couldn't help looking over her shoulder at the wooded area behind the shops. It was town property, officially – an overgrown man-made pond to hold storm water run-off. But the fence around it was cut down years ago.

Val smiled to herself. She, Ellie and cousin Ronnie – before her cousin's family moved away – used to play back there.

It wasn't dangerous. It was a small forest with a clean pond in the middle. But to the three girls, it was a vast wood and a crystal-clear lake, full of magic and wonder.

She remembered climbing a gnarly tree twenty paces from the fence. She and Ronnie sat on a thick branch and watched Ellie play wildly beneath them, shooting invisible arrows from her invisible bow, taking out scores of trolls and demons.

"I wish we didn't have to move," Ronnie said. She picked at the bark on the branch beside her.

"It's not very far," Val said. "Dad says we can drive there in like eight hours. Or we can fly there in like ten minutes."

"I don't think it's quite that quick," Ronnie said.

Below them, Ellie had apparently switched sides. She skidded to a stop, sending up a flurry of fallen leaves. "Elven fiends!" she called as she trained the imaginary bow on the cousins in the tree. "Now you die!"

* * *

Valarie's house was second from the next corner. It stood among the other houses on Birch Street, the only house that hadn't been renovated beyond recognition.

It stood like a relic. The house was tall and narrow. Its slate-blue paint was sun-bleached and cracked. The windows, no doubt original to the house, were warped and smudged. Their many panes caught the falling sun and seemed to glow from the inside.

"It has *charm*," Mum always said.

But everyone else thought it had *creepiness*.

A silver saloon car – sleek and shining new – sat in the driveway, sort of like putting a shimmering party dress on a warthog.

There was a lot to be jealous of when it came to cousin Ronnie. She lived in Chicago instead of this dinky little suburb. Her dad drove a cool-looking expensive car instead of a rust-red estate car, which Val's parents had bought before Val was even born. They even went on European holidays every year.

The front door of the Stoll house stood ajar, and the rickety screen door creaked when Val pulled it open. She cringed.

"There she is!" Aunt Jackie practically leapt up from the sofa. Her mum's sister was a nice enough woman, and a lot like Mum sometimes.

Then again, she did marry Uncle Anton. Val had never seen a more sinister-looking man. He always wore black, and his little black beard grew to a point from his chin. He stood and looked down his nose at Valarie, his beard pointed at her like a sabre.

"Hi, Jackie," Val said, letting herself be enveloped in the tall woman's lean, sinewy arms. She smelled like vanilla and grapefruit. "My *goodness*, I cannot believe how big you are!"

Val tried to smile and ended up smirking. "Hi, Anton," Val said, barely raising one hand in a wave.

He bowed his head slightly, sat down again, and pulled his phone from the inside pocket of his black suit jacket.

"So, where's Ronnie?" Val said, idly leaning against the arm of the sofa as Jackie sat beside her husband.

"I don't know," Jackie said, as if recalling something.

"You sent her out to the car to fetch her duffel," Anton said without looking away from his screen.

"That's right," Jackie said. "And then I asked her to take it up to your room. You're to be roommates all weekend, you know."

"Oh, I know," Val said.

"Of course, that was nearly an hour ago," Jackie said. "I can't imagine what's keeping her."

Val glared at Jackie in disbelief. "She's been up in my room for an *hour*?!" Val said. "Alone?!"

"Why, yes," Jackie said, a quizzical look on her face. "Isn't that all right? She *is* your cousin, after all."

"My *deranged* cousin," Val muttered as she ran up the narrow, steep stairs.

CHAPTER THREE

Music pulsed from behind Val's closed bedroom door. What the heck was Ronnie doing in there?

Val threw open the door, for once pleased that Mum and Dad still hadn't installed a lock for her. "Put it back!" she shouted, for there on her double bed sat her cousin Ronnie Vanster, and in her lap was Val's diary.

Open at the middle.

Val had never moved so fast. She snatched the book away, checked what page Ronnie had reached, and slammed it closed.

"I cannot believe you."

"Really?" Ronnie said, leaning back on her elbows. "Because you've known me for a long time, and to be honest this absolutely seems like something I'd do."

"It's just an expression," Val said as she placed her diary back in its hiding place. She'd have to choose a new hiding place for it later. "In this case it means, *you have betrayed my trust.*"

"Don't worry about it," Ronnie said, rising from the bed as the sun went down. "Your life is a bore anyway."

Ronnie had had her dark hair cut very short since Val saw her last Christmas, nearly a year ago. It made her look older than her fifteen years.

"Thanks," Val said. She spotted the shining green pendant on the silver thread of Ronnie's necklace. "Hey, I have the same – That *is* mine. Take it off."

"Caught me again!" Ronnie said. She unclasped the necklace and held it out to Val. "I would have given it back, you know. I'm not a thief."

"Sure." Val hung the necklace from its hook among her other jewellery on the wardrobe door. Nothing else seemed to be missing.

"I don't even think it's real," Ronnie said. She stood next to Val and looked at the necklaces hanging there. Most of them were like the one Ronnie had taken: silver chains, whisper thin, with a stone set in an organic-looking silver frame.

"Of course it is," Val said. She tapped the stone on each necklace: "Sapphire, emerald, onyx, agate, amethyst and ruby."

Ronnie shook her head. "Fakes."

"Whatever," Val said, shoving Ronnie gently aside and closing the wardrobe.

"Trust me," Ronnie said. "I happen to be very into crystals and gemstones. They have tremendous power, you know."

Val opened the bedroom door and pointed to the stairs. "Out."

"I'm hurt!" Ronnie said, faking offence.

"Just go," Val said, and she followed Ronnie to the stairs, closing her bedroom door behind her.

"By the way," Ronnie said, "the poems in your diary are actually pretty good."

"That's private," Val snapped.

"Whatever," Ronnie said, hurrying down the steps as Val walked slowly behind her.

"But thanks," Val added quietly.

CHAPTER FOUR

Val's parents served dinner in the dining room that night – the nice plates, the cloth napkins, the good silverware. Dad even set up some candles on the sideboard and dimmed the light that dangled over the table.

Even though they were just having takeaway fried chicken.

In the flickering orange glow, Uncle Anton looked creepier than ever. Even Ronnie, sitting right opposite Val, had a sinister air. Maybe it was the lighting, or maybe it just ran in the family.

That side of the family.

"So, Valarie," Jackie said as she cut with a knife and fork into her fried chicken drumstick.

Next to Val, her little brother, Edwin, held his own drumstick by the ankle and gnawed on it like a dog on a bone.

"We haven't seen you in *ages*," Jackie went on, still engaged in her chicken surgery. "How's school?"

The favourite question of grown-ups the world over, Val had to assume. And how exactly should she respond? With an in-depth description of her academic challenges? With a rundown of the social hierarchy of the school canteen? With a tearful spoken-word performance about her personal problems?

"Fine," Val said. That would do.

"Well, Ronnie has been having a lot of trouble at school," Jackie said.

"*Mum,*" Ronnie snapped.

Jackie was undeterred. "She could use some influence from a girl like you," she said to Val, ignoring her daughter's protests.

Ronnie laughed once, sarcastic and vile.

Val glared at her, but Ronnie kept her eyes on her food and a smirk on her face.

"You know," said Val's mum, "I wonder if Ronnie would actually be the better influence. She seems like such a *fun* young woman."

"*Mum!*" Val protested. She mentally noted the parallel relationships at the table.

"Oh, shush," Mum said, waving off her daughter's interjection. "I'm telling you, Ronnie. Valarie is up in her room doing heaven knows what for hours at a time – even weekends. Saturday nights!"

"So what?" Val said, pushing bright green peas around her plate with her fork. "I like being alone sometimes."

"Sometimes?" Mum said, half smiling, but

she wasn't even half joking. This wasn't the first time Mum had expressed concern about how much time Val spent alone.

"I see nothing wrong with spending time alone," Uncle Anton said. Though he spoke quietly, his rich voice seemed to require full attention. "It gives one time to think, to process and to plan."

No one spoke for a long, uncomfortable moment.

Finally, Val's dad broke the silence. "Maybe the girls can get out of the house tomorrow," he said. "See a film or something?"

Val and Ronnie looked at each other, and Val couldn't tell if the frost on Ronnie's face was directed towards her or their parents. The way Ronnie's eyes narrowed and nostrils flared, Val wasn't sure she wanted to find out.

"I don't need *help* to have fun," Val said. She felt her face going hot as she looked back and forth between her mum and dad. "I'm *fine.*"

"Calm down, honey," Dad said. "No one is saying you *need* help."

Calm down. Was anything ever more infuriating to hear, especially from the people driving you crazy to begin with?

"I'm finished," Val said, rising from the table.

"Already?" Mum said. "You've hardly touched your chicken."

"I'm not hungry." Val took her plate to the kitchen, left it next to the sink, and hurried to her room.

Behind her closed door, Val relaxed with a few deep breaths and pulled out her diary. That just made her angry again, so she threw her pen across the room and dropped her diary on the floor as she lay back on her bed.

She stared at the ceiling. Directly above

her were the remnants of an old poster that had once hung there. She'd torn it down in a fit of fury – years ago, now – and had never bothered to get up there and pull out the tacks, still clinging with fragments of the poster's corners.

She laughed to herself. She couldn't even remember what was on the poster. Some boy band she outgrew? No. It couldn't have been that.

Some childish cartoon characters, maybe? No . . . that didn't seem right either.

Her thoughts were interrupted by a firm knock at her door.

That'll be Dad, Val thought. He always was the one to come upstairs and talk to her when there'd been an incident like the one at dinner that evening.

"I don't want to talk about it, Dad," Val called through the door. "I just need some alone time."

The doorknob turned and the door opened a crack. A heavily made-up eye and a toothy grin appeared. Ronnie.

"We don't have to talk," Ronnie said as she pushed the door open all the way and stepped inside. "But we are going to be roomies for the next two nights."

Val sighed. "Fine," she said. "But I *really* don't need your *fun* charity."

Ronnie sneered as she knelt next to her bag and unzipped it. "Don't worry about that," she said as she dug around in the bag. "Our parents wouldn't know fun if it slapped them in the face."

Val let herself smile. "What are you looking for?" she asked.

"Just getting out the necessities for tonight's sleepover," Ronnie said.

She pulled out a small red sack that looked like it was made of velvet. It was tied at the top with a slim length of leather. Then she put it down in the middle of the carpet.

Next Ronnie pulled out a wooden box, about the size of a textbook, and laid it down beside the small sack. Its top was decorated with ornate carvings. At first, the decoration appeared nothing more than abstract swirls and shapes, but after a moment, Val was able to see faces among the wild etchings – monstrous faces, nightmarish faces.

And they seemed to be looking – and laughing – at Val.

CHAPTER FIVE

"What kind of necessities are those, exactly?" Val asked as she sat up and scooted to the edge of the bed. Her hands trembled and her heart raced, but she forced the fear down; she didn't want to seem babyish in front of her big-city cousin.

Ronnie thought for a moment, her hands poised over the wooden box. "Spiritual necessities," she finally said, and then she opened the box.

Val leaned over for a better look as Ronnie pulled out the contents: a square of wood with hinges at one end and what looked like a tiny plastic table with a window in its middle, the planchette.

"A Ouija board?" Val said, feigning casual disdain. In fact she felt anything but casual. Her heart raced at the rush of memories of years past, sitting in the woods with Ellie and Ronnie, their hands clasped in a circle of three – a tiny coven.

They summoned demons from the ether. They spoke to the spirits who haunted the woods. They called to the dryads and water spirits who hid among the branches and hovered on the surface of their crystal-clear lake.

She laughed lightly and said, "I haven't seen one of those in years."

"And I bet you've *never* seen one like this," Ronnie said, unfolding the wooden board. As well as the alphabet and *yes* and *no*, its front bore decorations similar to the box's lid.

The board, as well as being carved beautifully, was made of several different tones of wood, from the letters in chocolate brown to the creatures' eyes in light-coffee tan to the decorative leaves along the edge in gleaming sunshine yellow.

Val had to admit – at least to herself – it was a very nice Ouija board. Whoever had made it was a true artist.

"Whatever," she said aloud, rolling onto her side and picking up her phone from the bedside table. "I'm really not into silly stuff like that anymore. It's so childish."

Ronnie laughed. "You?" she said with disbelief. "Is this the same girl who used to play in the woods with me behind the old shops?"

Val smirked and kept her eyes on her phone. It was as if her cousin was reading her mind.

"The girl who," Ronnie went on as she rose up onto her knees, "insisted that everyone call her 'Quel'danu', wood elf ranger general?"

Val let a little laugh pop from her lips. "It was Quel'*thanu*," she said. She'd forgotten that detail. "And she was a *high* elf, thank you very much."

Ronnie stood and bowed deeply. "Forgive me, highness," she said, and both girls laughed.

"Come on," Ronnie said, dropping back to the carpet and sitting cross-legged. "Don't you want to find out what kind of dark secrets this house holds?"

"*This* boring house?" Val said, finally lowering her phone. "What secrets could possibly be here? Those of the old lady who lived here for fifty years before my parents bought it?"

Ronnie's eyes went wide. "Did she die

here?" she asked, her voice whispery and sacred.

"Ugh, I don't know," Val said. "Morbid much?"

Ronnie nodded. "Always," she said.

"Very funny," Val said.

The girls sat silently for a few moments, listening to the creaks of the old house. Val imagined the old woman's spirit – draped in a knitted shawl, reading glasses hanging around her neck – drifting across the first floor landing just outside her bedroom door. She shivered.

"Seriously, cuz," Ronnie said. "This house must be like a hundred years old."

"A hundred and twenty-nine, actually," Val said.

"See?" Ronnie tapped the planchette. "Our dumb home in Chicago is three years old. *Three*. I have underwear older than our apartment."

Val laughed again and rolled onto her stomach to look down at the Ouija board.

"Have you ever seen or heard anything . . . *spooky* in the house?" Ronnie asked.

"No," Val said. She picked up her phone again to hide her eyes. "Not really."

It wasn't entirely true. She'd lived in this house most of her life – for all of her life she could remember, anyway. And when Val was little . . . well, sometimes a little kid's imagination gets the better of them.

That older girl in a white dress who played with Val in the basement playroom?

What was her name? Ana Petrikoven?

She was just pretend, an imaginary friend.

The monster with three horns and red eyes that lived in Val's wardrobe but only after bedtime?

He wouldn't let me get up in the night to go to the toilet.

That was just a bad dream.

The scratching at the walls just beside her bedroom window on the darkest, rainiest nights, when all the foul creatures wanted to get in from the rain?

They crawled up the walls outside and clawed at the lock on her window to come in out of the storm – and to have some little girl for a midnight snack.

No, that was just the skinny branches of the overgrown elm rubbing against the walls of the house.

"Ugh, Val," Ronnie said, sagging with disappointment. "Your parents were right. You are no fun."

With that, she pushed the Ouija board to the side, grabbed her toothbrush from her duffel, and headed to the bathroom to get ready for bed.

Val lowered her phone and sighed. Her chest felt heavy and her breath was short. All of Val's self-doubts – about fantasy stories, magic and playing childish games – bubbled up from her stomach like bile. Ronnie's visit would be harder to navigate than she'd thought.

CHAPTER SIX

Val dreamed she was in the woods. She knew it was the woods behind the row of shops, but the trees seemed to go on forever in every direction. She wore her green elf robe, just like she had years ago playing with Ronnie.

It fit her well. She lowered her hood and felt the howling wind on her ears. She heard every sound for miles: a cracking twig, the tender footsteps of a young doe, the gentle snore of a bear in its den.

"Valarie."

Val sat up in bed. Her room was lit only by the glow of the clock beside her bed – 2:30 in the morning.

Had someone called out to her? On the floor beside her bed, Ronnie lay in a sleeping bag, her head off her pillow and her mouth open, fast asleep.

"Valarie."

It was hardly more than a whisper, and it couldn't be Ronnie. Val was staring right at her; she was definitely asleep.

She pushed off her covers and slipped quietly off the bed, taking care not to bump her cousin.

All the lights in the house were off. Only the automatic nightlight in the bathroom lit the first floor landing.

"Dad?" Val whispered into the darkness. "Mum, is that you?"

She moved slowly across the carpeted landing and pressed her ear to her parents' bedroom door. She heard the soft sound of her father's snoring and the whistle of wind through their open window.

"Valarie." The voice grew more urgent, and she could tell now that it wasn't coming from her parents' room. It wasn't coming from Edwin's room across the landing. Nor, thankfully, was it coming from downstairs, where Uncle Anton and Aunt Jackie were sleeping on the sofabed.

It came from above her.

Val looked up at the square hatch in the ceiling. A slim rope hung down from there with a knob of wood at its end. She wrapped her fingers around the rope and tugged.

The hatch opened slowly, and from within a stout wooden ladder unfolded, like the ramp of an alien ship upon landing on earth.

The ladder's feet settled silently on the carpet, and Val went up.

It had been years since Val had been

up here. She remembered old cardboard boxes, dusty baby furniture, Mum's old collection of CDs. But tonight, the attic was nearly empty, its plain wooden floor pale with dust and stretching out from the hatch so much further than Val could have imagined.

The only thing in the attic – besides Val's head, poking up from the hatch – was a doll's house under the little window under the furthest dormer.

"Valarie."

"Who's there?" she whispered into the dusty dank, though it was clear no one was there at all.

She climbed the rest of the way and, on hands and knees, moved across the dusty floor towards the doll's house. She didn't want to, at least not exactly. A part of her – in her stomach and in her chest, which burned with anxiety – wanted to do anything but crawl to the doll's house.

Still she was drawn to it, like she was no longer in control of her arms and legs. They pulled her forwards.

The doll's house looked so familiar. A tiny voice inside her mind screamed, *Stop! Stop!* But she crawled on.

As she reached the doll's house, she realized why it had looked familiar: it was an exact copy of her own house, except much smaller. The outside walls, where they weren't cut away, were the same slate blue of her house.

The kitchen shined with new stainless steel appliances. A red stand mixer sat on the little granite worktop. A flatscreen TV hung above the cherry mantelpiece in the living room.

Val crouched in front of the little house. Her gaze moved across the furnishings and up the narrow stairs. She found her parents' bedroom, the little bed's blankets and sheets rumpled and wrinkled. She found Edwin's small room, with the funny little racing car bed and the lamp that looked like a bat and ball.

And across the landing, with the door standing open, was her room, and she gasped.

She leaned over the top of the house for a closer look. On the floor of her miniature bedroom lay an unrolled powder-blue sleeping bag. A doll with short black hair slept inside.

On the bed, another doll – this one with long brown hair – slept beneath a floral print pink cover.

Val's cover. And the doll could only be Val. She reached down to pull back the covers to see the doll's face–

"Valarie." The whisper again, this time much closer. The voice seemed to come from the tiny bedroom's wardrobe.

Valarie reached one shaking hand into the doll's house, half expecting the house itself to chomp her hand off, and pulled open the tiny wardrobe door. Inside was a third doll, and Val pinched it between two fingers and pulled it out.

It was grotesque, a monster with a face like one of the demonic images on Ronnie's Ouija board. It had a nasty, stained smile of sharp little teeth, and beady yellow-green eyes that seemed to stare right back at Val.

Thick, matted hair, caked with mud, covered its little body, and its ears were tall and pointy.

And it smelled. It reeked like dry mud and rotten eggs and dirty copper pennies.

"Valarie," the doll whispered once again.

She squinted at its tiny mouth.

"Valarie."

The tiny mouth didn't move. The smell grew stronger. Val turned around, and the very same monster towered over her as she knelt – and screamed.

* * *

Val sat up in bed, her breathing ragged, her chest tight, and a cold, prickly sweat rising all over her body.

"You OK?" said Ronnie, also sitting up.

"It was a dream," Val said to herself.

"I thought so," Ronnie said. She rubbed her eyes with her fists and curled up inside her sleeping bag. "Go back to sleep."

Val lay in her bed and stared at the ceiling, struggling to recall images from her nightmare. Most of it had faded quickly from her memory. She was certain only that somehow it was Ronnie's fault. Her cousin had filled her head with ridiculous ideas right before bedtime, after all.

Val rolled onto her side and pulled her covers up to her chin. She stared across the dark bedroom.

Ronnie was already asleep again. Her soft, slow breathing helped Val relax for a moment.

Then she remembered the wardrobe door.

The dream was still fuzzy, but she knew that something terrifying waited behind that wardrobe door.

"Come on, Val," she whispered to herself. "You're acting like a child. There are no *monsters* in the real world."

She swung her legs off the side of the bed and, careful not to step on her cousin, crossed the room on tiptoes. The wardrobe door stood ajar. It always did. It stuck too much to close all the way.

She wrapped her fingers around the doorknob and took a deep breath. Steeling herself, she pulled the door wide open in one quick motion.

Clothes. A small set of drawers. Her

jewellery box. On the shelf above her head, a plastic tub of old, childish toys.

"There," she said to herself, and she closed the wardrobe. "Nothing to be afraid of at all."

She quietly got back into bed and fell quickly to sleep.

CHAPTER SEVEN

Val woke to sunshine on her face and the sound of the shower on the other side of the wall by her head. Ronnie's sleeping bag was empty.

For a brief moment, the sunlight felt warm and comforting. The sound of the shower felt homely and safe.

Val sat up and stretched, and when she opened her eyes, the wardbrobe door brought everything back to her mind.

Her heart thumped twice. Her stomach

lurched. She dropped from the bed and pulled open Ronnie's duffel bag.

"I have to see what other dark magic she's brought into this house," Val muttered to herself.

She pulled out the small red sack and dumped out its contents: crystals, all shapes and sizes and colours. She ran her hand over them, feeling their cool and sharp edges and smooth, glassy faces.

She picked up the sack and turned it over in her hands. In gold lettering on its bottom were the words *Windy City Toys, Magic and Games*.

"A toy shop?" Val whispered to herself. She knew Chicago, where Ronnie lived now, was nicknamed the Windy City.

She grabbed the Ouija box and turned it over. Sure enough, carved into the wooden bottom and painted gold, it read *Windy City Toys, Magic and Games*.

"It's nothing but a fancy toy," she said aloud. "There's no real magic here."

"Well, duh," Ronnie said as she came in. She was wrapped in a heavy-looking black dressing gown. In gold, the initials V.V. were stitched into the chest.

Val had been so absorbed in snooping she hadn't heard the shower turn off. "Oh, I was just–," Val started, but then she dropped back on her haunches and crossed her arms. "Whatever. You snooped through my stuff too."

Ronnie shrugged and sat on the carpet facing Val. "Doesn't bother me," she said. "I have nothing to hide."

Ronnie's black hair, towelled dry, stood up in wild spikes all over. She looked like some kind of wild beast. Her wicked grin was the final piece of the accidental costume.

Val picked up the bag of gems and crystals. "So this stuff is just junk?"

"Oh, I wouldn't say that," Ronnie said. "To me, with magical items, you get out of them what you put in."

"What the heck does *that* mean?" Val said.

"It means, dear cousin," Ronnie said as she narrowed her eyes and her mouth bent into a razor thin smile, "that if you believe these things are magic, then they are."

Val put down the bag of crystals and leaned against her bed. She thought about her dream and how real it had seemed. She remembered how strongly she once believed in magic. But did she still believe?

"If I tell you something, will you promise not to laugh?" Val said.

"I'm not big on promises," Ronnie said, crossing her arms. "Then again I'm not big on laughing, either. I'm more of a wicked-grin kind of girl."

Val took a deep breath. Then, as quickly as she could but leaving out as little as possible, she told her cousin about her dream.

"So then I woke up," Val finished, "and I was convinced your magic was the cause of my nightmare."

"Hence the snooping," Ronnie said.

Val nodded.

Ronnie sat quietly for a moment, her eyes a million miles away. But she definitely didn't laugh. She didn't even grin.

Suddenly she jumped to her feet. "Let's go," she said.

"Go where?" Val asked, looking up at Ronnie.

"That wasn't just a nightmare," Ronnie said. "I know you, Val. I know deep inside, you really believe in magic, and I think this weird old house knows that. I think it was speaking to you, trying to tell you something."

"So what am I supposed to do about it?" Val asked.

"Listen to it," Ronnie said. "Come with me to check out the attic."

CHAPTER EIGHT

"I thought you said the attic was empty," Ronnie said.

The girls stalked through the dusty attic, their heads low to avoid smacking against the beams that crossed the underside of the roof.

"In my dream it was," Val said. "I haven't been up here in years."

"Where was the doll's house?" Ronnie asked.

Val turned slowly to get her bearings. Dim grey light filtered through the dust coating the window in the far dormer.

"There," she said, pointing. "Under the window."

"It's not there now," Ronnie said. She began digging through boxes and poking behind an old set of drawers.

Val crossed to the window anyway and looked out. It was a gloomy morning, and rain fell in sheets against the outside of the window. She hadn't noticed it before, but she could hear the incessant drumming of raindrops on the roof just over her head.

"Ooh, an old photo of your mum," Ronnie said behind her. "She had glasses?!"

Val ignored her and leaned her forehead against the window to peer into the back garden. The huge elm tree stood in the centre of the garden. There used to be a tyre swing there, when Val was little, but the rope had grown weak and frayed, and finally Dad had taken it down.

Even the worn spot where Val and Ellie's feet used to drag across the ground was gone.

A dark, hunched figure crossed the garden and disappeared behind the old tree's massive trunk.

Val flinched. Her eyes must have been playing tricks on her. She was just still jumpy from that nightmare.

"Whoa, what's *this*?" Ronnie asked from the other side of the attic. "Your dad was in a band?"

Val squinted, trying to find any sign of anyone through the pelting rain and swaying branches of the old tree. But who would be outside in this downpour?

Not even weird Uncle Anton would do that.

Through the branches, she saw the figure again. It moved quickly. It almost looked like nothing more than a shadow. A trick of the dim light and the wind through the tree.

"Valarie," said Ronnie from behind her. "You have to come and look at this."

But Val couldn't turn from the window even if she wanted to, because at that moment the shadowy figure stepped out in the open: the monster from Val's nightmare. Despite being hunched over, almost bent in half, it was tall and strong-looking. Thick, matted hair covered its body, and its pointy ears twitched like those of a dog on edge.

"Val, seriously," Ronnie said. Her voice sounded miles away. "Come and look at this."

As the monster moved across the garden, its head hanging low and swinging back and forth, it seemed to be looking for something.

Suddenly it stopped. Something caught its attention.

With a speed and grace that shocked Val, the foul beast stood tall and swung its gaze up the back of the house. Its eyes glowed as it found her there in the window, and it grinned, showing an impossible number of sharp, yellow fangs.

Val screamed and turned from the window to run, but Ronnie stood right behind her, her eyes big and sleepy and her mouth wide open.

"Val, look at this," she said. Or she seemed to say. In fact, her mouth never moved.

But it was Ronnie's voice, and it came again. "Val, you have to look at this."

Until she collapsed in a heap at Val's feet, and there stood the monster instead. It grinned at her as it had when it found her in the window. Its bright yellow-green eyes shone. The colour itself made her ill.

"Val," the monster said in her cousin's voice, "you have to look at this."

* * *

Val woke screaming and sat up in bed like a shot. Ronnie's sleeping bag was empty, and Val heard the white-noise rush of the shower through the wall.

She leaned over to push aside the curtain. It was a sunny morning. An autumn wind rustled the yellowing leaves of the big old elm tree, and what few clouds hung in the sky were as wispy and soft as candyfloss. But were they real, or was this another nightmare?

The shower turned off, and a moment later Ronnie burst into the room wrapped in Val's dressing gown, her hair dripping and her pyjamas bunched up in her arms.

"Good, you're up," Ronnie said. "Let's go shopping."

CHAPTER NINE

"I've missed this place," Ronnie said wistfully as the girls strolled slowly through the shopping centre.

"Really?" Val said. She couldn't imagine anyone missing this place. They'd been there over an hour already, and they'd gone into the same six shops Val always went into.

"How could you miss this when you live in a big city like Chicago?" Val asked.

"Hard to explain," Ronnie said. "For starters, it smells better here." She took a deep sniff as they passed Val's favourite cosmetics shop.

"Ooh, is that new?" Ronnie asked, suddenly picking up speed.

She headed for a shop called Blessed Be. The windows of its small shopfront displayed gems, old-looking books and a whisper-thin mannequin wrapped in shimmery scarves.

"I think so," Val said. She hurried after her cousin.

Inside, the place smelled strongly of incense. Ronnie spent some time browsing the gem case, but everything was pretty expensive.

"So is any of this stuff real?" Val asked. It occurred to her that she'd never *really* looked at Ronnie's magic stuff. That had been a dream. "Is *your* stuff real?"

"My stuff," Ronnie said, picking up a large and rugged-looking stone, "is from a toy shop in Chicago."

Then that part of the dream, at least, was real. Val wondered what else from the dream was real. She shivered at the remembered image of that foul monster, and of Ronnie collapsing on the attic floor.

Ronnie put down the rock. "So of course it's real," she added.

"Huh?" Val said. "But you just said it's from a toy shop."

"It's real if–," Ronnie began.

Val cut her off. "If you believe it's real." Then that, too, was true, just like she'd dreamed it.

"Yep," Ronnie said. She headed for the exit. Val trailed after her.

"I could pick up any old stone from your driveway," Ronnie said as they left the shop, "and use it for magical purposes if I believe in it and know what I'm doing."

"That makes sense," said a familiar voice.

A chill ran up Val's spine, and she turned to find Ellie, Olive and Mackenzie. They stood thick as thieves, each with at least three shopping bags and a sneer.

"Oh," Val said. "It's you."

"It's obvious I'd find you coming out of the *magic shop*," Ellie said. "Or should I say, the *tragic* shop."

Her friends laughed.

"Is that Ellie Roth?" Ronnie said, stepping around Val. "Wow. I haven't seen you in forever."

"Veronica?" Ellie said, taken slightly aback. She looked Val's cousin up and down.

"It's Ronnie now," she said. "And there's no real magic in *there*."

"Ronnie," Val hissed at her. "Don't."

"Don't what?" Ronnie said. She shot Val a wink. "Your friend Ellie's not allowed to hear about how things are done in the city?"

"What are you talking about?" Ellie said.

"In Chicago," Ronnie said. "Where I live now."

"So?" Ellie shot back.

"So," Ronnie said, striding casually closer to Ellie, "in Chicago, literally everyone I know is into real magic."

"Oh, please," Olive said.

Ellie shushed her. "What do you mean, real magic?" she asked, her voice serious and quiet.

Ronnie shrugged one shoulder. "Basic stuff, mostly," she said. "Summoning spells. Curses. Making contact with the dead."

"*You've* made contact with dead people?" Ellie asked.

"Um, obviously," Ronnie said.

"Ronnie, stop," Val said.

"No, no," Ellie said. "It's fine. Ronnie is

obviously a woman of the world."

"The *under*world," Olive said out of the side of her mouth.

"Guilty," Ronnie admitted.

"Listen," Ellie said, stepping closer to Ronnie. "I'm having a sleepover with these two" – she thumbed over her shoulder at Olive and Mackenzie – "tonight. Why don't you come too?"

Val tensed her shoulders.

"Nah, I'm hanging with my cousin tonight," Ronnie said.

Val sighed.

"Bring her too," Ellie said. "I mean, obviously."

"Oh, no no," Val said, grabbing Ronnie's elbow. "Really, it's fine."

"I insist," Ellie said.

"Me too," Ronnie agreed. Her grin grew, and she put an arm around Val's shoulders.

"We'll be there."

* * *

At home Val sat on her bed with her head in her hands. "I can't believe I let you do this," she said.

"Oh, come on," Ronnie said as she shoved a few things into her duffel. "It'll be fun. I can't believe you and Ellie aren't friends anymore. You two were inseparable."

"Well, we've separated," Val said. "Hey, what are you doing?"

"Packing," Ronnie said.

"I see that," Val said. "Why are you packing your Ouija board?"

"You saw how those mean girls reacted to my talk about magic and stuff," Ronnie said. "They'll love it."

"No way," Val said, literally putting her foot down. "No magic stuff. None. I do *not* want to have another nightmare, especially while I'm sleeping at Ellie's house!"

Ronnie set her with a defiant glare, but then her face softened. "Fine," she said. She pulled the Ouija box and the bag of gems out of her bag. "No magic."

"Thank you," Val said. "I wouldn't even be going, but the idea of spending a night alone in my own room is even more terrifying than sleeping at Ellie's."

CHAPTER TEN

"Well, as I live and breathe." Ellie Roth's mother stood in the open front door with a hand on her hip and looked at Val with her mouth hanging open. "Is this Valarie Stoll? And Veronica Vanster?"

"Hi, Heather," Val said. For as long as Val could remember, Ellie's mum had insisted on being called by her first name.

"I haven't seen you in just *ages*," Heather said. "You know, I ask Ellie. I say, 'When is Valarie coming over? It's been ages!' And she just says nothing. You know teenagers."

"I sure do," Val said.

Heather turned to Ronnie. "Didn't I hear your family moved to Chicago?"

"Yep," Ronnie said. "Just here for the holiday weekend."

Heather stepped to the side. "Well, the girls are in the family room, down in the basement," she said. "You remember the way, Val?"

"Yep!" Val said as she and Ronnie hurried in and down the hallway to the stairs. "Thanks!"

The Roths' house had a walkout basement, and from the family room a sliding door offered a beautiful view of the sloping lawn down to the creek.

It was dark now, though, and Val could see nothing in the big glass door apart from the reflection of the family room.

Mackenzie and Olive were already there. With Ellie between them, they sat together in the middle of the room. A white coffee table had been pushed against the wall, blocking a cupboard door.

"There you two are," Ellie said, shifting her legs beneath her. "You guys haven't eaten dinner yet, right?"

Val shook her head and followed Ronnie's lead by sitting on the floor with the other girls, creating a circle of five people.

It occurred to Val that they were in the shape of a pentagon, or the points of a pentagram. She shivered, but chased the notion from her mind.

There's no such thing as magic, she thought as hard as she could, *or monsters.*

"Dad!" Ellie shouted, and Val jumped.

Ronnie shot Val a look, like *Are you OK?*

"Are you home with the pizza yet?" Ellie called.

Val shook her head and mouthed, *I'm fine.*

Mr Roth came down the stairs carrying a pizza box and five cans of flavoured sparkling water. "Here we go," he said. He still had his jacket on.

"Thanks, Mr Roth," Val said. The other girls said nothing.

"You're very welcome, Valarie," Mr Roth said. "And may I say what a pleasure it is to see you around these parts again!"

"Dad," Ellie said as she took the box from him, put it in the centre of their pentagon, and opened it. "You're embarrassing me."

Mr Roth put the sparkling water down quickly and headed back upstairs.

* * *

After they'd eaten and watched a film – Ellie had insisted on a scary one – the girls changed into their pyjamas. Val and Ronnie were first back to the middle of the family room.

Ronnie had a little velvet sack in her lap.

"Ronnie!" Val said, aghast. "You said . . ."

"Don't worry," Ronnie said, leaning over. She lifted the bag and showed her the toy shop logo on its bottom. "Remember? Just junk, like you said."

"But you said– " Val started.

Ronnie cut her off. "But we *don't* believe, do we?" she whispered and winked.

"I suppose," Val said.

"Good," Ronnie said. "Now we'll have some fun with your former friends."

"What do you have in mind?" Val asked, nervous and a little excited. Maybe it *was* time to get back at Ellie Roth.

"Just a little fright," Ronnie said. "Once I have the seance going, you quietly make your way upstairs and around the back. Wait outside the patio door there." She nodded towards the sliding glass doors that led to the Roths' back garden.

"Then what?" Val asked.

"When I give the signal," Ronnie said, "open the door and scream 'Rawr' or something. They will absolutely *die*."

The others came back, still in whispers.

Before anyone could speak, Ronnie held up the bag, shook it and dumped the stones onto the rug in front of her.

"Now," she said, her voice low and raspy, "let's find out what secrets this house holds."

"None, I bet," Ellie said. Her loud and brash voice shattered the solemn mood.

Ronnie hummed quietly as she hovered one hand over the gems and crystals. She closed her eyes. "Dim the lights," she said quickly.

Olive leapt to her feet, eyes wide, and hurried to oblige.

"If there is a spirit here," Ronnie said to the darkness as Olive sat back down, "please favour us with your voice."

Nothing happened.

Val held her breath and watched her cousin.

Ronnie rubbed her hand over the gems now, rolling them across the pile of the rug. She hummed as she did.

"What are you doing?" Mackenzie asked in a cynical whisper.

Ronnie didn't reply. She just kept humming and running her hand over the crystals.

"She's finding the correct harmonic to speak to the, um, deceased," Val said nervously. She hoped the rasp of her whisper would hide the shaking in her voice.

"I hear them," Ronnie said. She closed her hand over a crystal – a dark blue one – and held it close to her chest.

"Spirits!" she called, her voice loud and

confident. "Please share your voice with us!"

"This is stupid," Ellie said.

"Shh," Olive hissed.

"They're nearby," Ronnie said. She opened her eyes and opened her fist. The blue crystal in her palm glowed.

"Whoa," Mackenzie said.

"Big whoop," Ellie said. "An LED."

"Please forgive her, spirits," Ronnie said, her face towards the ceiling. "She does not believe. Please, share your voice with her!"

The other girls looked up at the ceiling too, and Ronnie quickly glanced at Val. She nodded towards the steps.

"Oh," Val said, standing up. "I have to, um, go to the loo."

No one paid her any attention. She slipped out, subtly unlocking the sliding door as she passed it.

She hurried up the stairs and found the main floor dark. The Roths must have gone up to bed already.

The front door had the same old lock as the one at her house. She opened it with a quiet click and a pop and went out into the night, making sure she'd left it unlocked – just in case.

The grass was damp with dew, and in a few moments her feet and the hems of her pyjama bottoms were soaking wet and cold.

Val made her way in the dark to the back garden, nearly slipping on the damp slope. She reached the sliding door and looked in, making sure she stayed back from the glass so they wouldn't see her.

Even with the lights dimmed, she could easily see what was going on in the room. Ronnie sat facing her. The other girls sat angled so she couldn't see their faces at all.

Now Ronnie held two more crystals, and they all glowed.

Ellie was probably right. Just an LED light in a hunk of plastic from the toy shop.

It was cold. Summer was barely behind her, but already the nights were cold. She hugged herself against the chill, but it did no good.

She jogged in place and stared at Ronnie. "Come on, come on," she whispered to herself. "Give me the signal already."

Five minutes passed. "What is taking so long?" Val muttered to herself. "Forget this. I'm freezing."

She put a hand on the door's handle to slide it open, but at the same moment, the girls inside all jumped. Olive put a hand over her open mouth.

"I guess she's finally starting the real scares now," Val said. In spite of the cold, she watched closely, eagerly. "What are they looking at?"

The cupboard door. The four girls – even Ronnie, who had to twist in place – watched the cupboard door.

Then she saw why – it was shaking. It rattled against that little coffee table as if someone – or something – was inside and trying to get out.

"How is she doing that?" Val said to herself.

In front of her, the girls backed slowly from the cupboard. Then, *boom!*

The door slammed fully open, sending the little coffee table tumbling onto its side.

The girls – all of them shrieking in fear – jumped to their feet and fled the basement, up the stairs.

"What the–" Val said, and she pulled the sliding door's handle.

It didn't budge. Someone had locked it.

"Oh, come *on*," Val said. She was beginning

to think *she* was the one being pranked tonight after all.

She thumped a fist on the glass. "Ronnie!" she called. "Open the door, please. Joke's over."

Val expected the four girls to come back down the basement steps at any second, laughing at what a fool she was. She wasn't even surprised that Ronnie had decided to make Val the stooge after being friends with Ellie, Mackenzie and Olive for no more than three hours.

Cool, mean girls click with cool, mean girls, and Val would never be a girl like that. A part of her would always be the high elf ranger playing in the woods.

Honour. Magic. Nature. *Fantasy.*

The girls didn't come back downstairs. Instead, a dim green light began to shine from inside the cupboard.

Two green lights. Yellowish.

Eyes.

The hulking figure moved slowly out of the dark impossible depths of the cupboard, from its own wicked dimension and into this one.

It stepped into the family room and stood there, its huge head swaying slowly, its ears twitching and straining. Listening. Sniffing. Searching for *her.*

Val held her breath and backed away from the door, but she couldn't take her eyes off the monster.

But the tiny motion of backing away was all it needed. It snapped to face the sliding door.

And it found her.

CHAPTER ELEVEN

It was impossible. No one could see through this door when it was dark outside.

But the beast's wicked-looking mouth stretched into a horrifying grin. Its sickening green eyes found Val's. It definitely saw her.

Val turned and ran for the front of the house, thankful that she'd left the front door unlocked. The girls would be in the kitchen probably, waiting for her to come upstairs so they could laugh at her.

She had to warn them. She had to let them know the monster was in the basement.

She slipped on the wet slope, falling against the shrubbery. She pushed herself up again, her hands now caked in mud and compost, and ran again. She banged her toe on a stone garden edging at the corner and struggled to run through the pain.

The monster might smash through the sliding glass door any second now.

Or maybe it was already halfway up the basement stairs.

As Val finally reached the front door, it flung open.

Val flinched in the bright light of the front hallway. After so long in the darkness of the back garden, it was too bright. Tears sprung to her eyes at once.

The other girls stood there, Ronnie in the centre, with Ellie, Olive and Mackenzie standing around her with their phones out, snapping pictures and laughing. Ronnie frowned.

"Oh man," Mackenzie said, shaking her head as she no doubt hurried to post the photo online, "she's actually *crying*."

Val quickly wiped her eyes with the back of her hand and shoved through the gaggle of girls. It was all a prank, and Val was the victim.

Once again, Ellie and her friends had found a way to make her a laughing stock, and this time her dear cousin had joined in too, just for good measure.

But the monster . . . How could they have–?

"Wait a second, Val," Ronnie said, chasing after her. She blocked the steps to the basement.

"Why should I?" Val said. She backed against the wall and crossed her arms.

"Look, I didn't even mean for that to happen," Ronnie said, her face close to Val's. "But Olive saw you unlock the patio door, and . . . well . . ."

"You decided to pull a switcheroo on me?" Val snapped.

"It wasn't my idea," Ronnie said. "It was Ellie's."

"It was a mean idea," Val said. "And it was freezing out there."

"I'm sorry," Ronnie said. "I really am."

"How did you even do that?" Val said.

Ronnie made a confused face and held up one hand. A length of floss was wrapped around her fingers in a tangled mess. "How'd I shake the door?" she asked. "With this. I thought it was pretty obvious."

"No, not that," Val said. "The other thing."

Ronnie thought for a moment. "You mean the glowing crystals?" she said, sounding a little surprised at how dense Val was being.

"No!" Val said, but before she could go on, Ellie stepped up to them.

"I'm sorry too," she said. "It *was* mean of me."

"Oh, please," Olive said. "She was going to scare us. We scared her. Fair play."

Ellie shook her head. "But we ganged up on her," she said. "That's much worse."

"Whatever," Mackenzie said, sliding past Ronnie and heading downstairs.

"Wait!" Val said. "Don't go down there! It's–"

The four girls turned to look at her, Mackenzie halfway down the basement steps.

"It's what?" Ronnie prodded.

"Nothing," Val said after a moment. "Never mind."

"She was just trying to scare you, Mack," Olive said as she followed Mackenzie down the steps. "Trying to get back at you. Nice try, Valadork."

"Good one," Val said, rolling her eyes.

Ellie hurried downstairs too.

Val half expected to hear the three mean girls scream and the sound of a thousand fangs crunching on mean girl bones.

Instead she just heard whispers and giggles. Maybe she was just losing her mind . . . as well as her friends.

"I really am sorry," Ronnie said. "Let's just forget about it, OK? Let's get some sleep."

But Val couldn't sleep. She lay on the sofa on her side with her eyes on the cupboard door. It was closed tight, again blocked by the little coffee table.

And, Val chided herself, *monsters are* not *real.*

CHAPTER TWELVE

In the morning, Val left with hardly a word to the other girls. Ronnie, after rushing through goodbyes and thank-yous, hurried after her.

"Still angry?" Ronnie said.

Val glared at her and walked faster.

"I'll take that as a yes," Ronnie called after her.

Val's mum opened the front door before the girls reached the driveway.

"Good morning, girls," Mum said, standing

in the open doorway. "My goodness, Val! You look positively worn out!"

She took Val's overnight bag and put it just inside.

"That's because I didn't sleep at all," Val said.

"She slept a little, Aunt Dee," Ronnie said. "I promise."

Val collapsed onto the sofa. "Tell *Aunt Dee* about your little joke last night," Val said.

"It was really nothing," Ronnie said. She sat on the sofa at Val's feet and playfully smacked her on the leg. "Your daughter is overreacting. The other girls and I gave her a little scare, that's all."

"You call that a little scare?" Val said, sitting up in anger. "And that's to say nothing of those rats Mackenzie and Olive taking photos to embarrass me!"

"Oh, honey," Mum said. She sat on the arm of the sofa and put a hand on her arm.

Val tugged it away.

"That's how friends are sometimes," Mum said. "Especially at your age. It's not ideal, I suppose, but it's part of belonging to a group of friends."

"See?" Ronnie said. "It wasn't *that* big a deal."

"Whatever," Val said. "*Those* girls are *not* my friends. But apparently Ronnie is their new bestie."

Mum clucked her tongue as she rose and went into the kitchen. Val saw her father, aunt and uncle at the round table. Before the door swung closed again, Anton's beady dark eyes caught hers. She thought he smiled.

Ronnie got up too, but Val grabbed her wrist.

"I didn't tell you everything last night," Val said.

"What?" Ronnie said.

"There's a reason I'm 'overreacting', as you put it," Val said, "but I wasn't sure until just now."

"Just tell me what you're talking about," Ronnie said impatiently.

"When I was scared," Val said. "It wasn't just the cupboard door banging open and being alone in the dark. I . . . I saw the monster again."

"'Again'?" Ronnie said. "What do you mean, 'again'? What monster?"

"The one I saw–" She cut herself off. "Oh. I didn't tell you. That was in my dream too."

"Maybe you should back up," Ronnie said.

So Val did. She told her about every scary thing that she'd seen since Ronnie had arrived, right up to the monster stepping out of the dark depths of Ellie's basement cupboard.

Ronnie looked pale. She grabbed her bag

and ran upstairs without a word.

Val chased her. When she reached her bedroom, Ronnie was on the bed, flicking through one of her occult books.

"Look at this," Ronnie said.

Val sat beside her and Ronnie dropped the open book in her lap.

A pen-and-ink drawing stared up at her: the monster, right down to the wicked, toothy grin. The only thing missing was the yellow-green of its eyes.

"That's it," Val said as the little hairs on the back of her neck stood up. "That's the monster."

"I was afraid of that," Ronnie said. She unzipped her duffel and pulled out the sack of gems. She dumped the contents onto the covers between them.

Most were like the LED ones. Now that Val could see them closely, they were all obviously fake. Just hunks of plastic. She could even see where the machine had clipped each one from a huge set of probably thousands it moulded at one time.

But one stood out. It wasn't the brightest in colour. It wasn't the largest or the smallest. It wasn't even the most beautiful. In fact, it was rather plain.

Among the rest, this one crystal was a pale yellow-green, almost mustardy. It was oddly shaped, as if it had grown naturally in a cave somewhere.

And it didn't shine. While every stone in the bag shone, and every stone in Val's jewellery box shone, this one just sat there, looking dull and heavy and old.

"Where did *that one* come from?" Val said, since it obviously didn't come from Windy City Toys, Magic and Games. She picked it up. It was rough, with sharp corners, like it had broken off of a much larger stone.

Ronnie, her hands shaking, took the stone from Val and stared at it. "We went to Germany this summer," Ronnie said.

"Yeah, I know," Val said. "You always go on amazing trips."

"Just – just listen," Ronnie snapped, glaring at her. "Dad dragged us all over the countryside, looking at antique shops and weird little places run by weird little people.

"This one shop," Ronnie went on, "in a village so tiny I'm not sure it even counts as a village, was built right into the side of a mountain, so inside it was dark and cold and smelled like soil and sulphur.

"The woman who ran it was barely tall enough to see over her own counter," Ronnie said as she turned her head to stare out of the window at the grey morning. "She wore a long dress, so when she walked across the dirt floor, she almost seemed to glide.

"Dad found nothing he wanted," Ronnie

said after a beat. "But I found this." She held up the yellow crystal, almost like an afterthought. "And I bought it. It cost almost nothing. The shop lady seemed almost happy to be rid of it."

She turned to face her cousin and added, "Now I see that she probably was."

CHAPTER THIRTEEN

"I don't get it," Val admitted.

"She told me," Ronnie said. "Or she tried. But her English wasn't great, and Dad's German is . . . also not great. But she said it contains the *alp*."

"Like, the mountain?" Val said.

"No," Ronnie explained. "It's German for 'elf', but not the elves that help Santa Claus and not the elves that Frodo Baggins travelled with, either."

"That would be far more pleasant," Val said.

"From what it says in that book," Ronnie went on, "if it started out appearing in a nightmare, and then appeared to you at Ellie's house, it must be getting stronger.

"Soon it will be outside of the crystal entirely," Ronnie concluded.

"That doesn't sound good," Val said, staring at the nightmarish ink drawing on her lap.

"No," Ronnie said, "but it's not hopeless. I know how to kill it."

* * *

The day dragged after that. Neither girl could eat or sit still for more than a moment as they waited for nightfall.

While their parents seemed chipper and lively as they went to lunch, saw a film and laughed over dinner, Val and Ronnie sulked and fidgeted and bounced their knees.

Finally, darkness fell. The girls got ready

for bed and shut themselves inside Val's bedroom.

"How do we know it'll come here?" Val asked. "Maybe it'll turn up at Ellie's house again."

Ronnie shook her head. "No," she said. "It's focused on you."

"Why?" Val asked, surprised to find she was on the verge of tears.

Ronnie scooted next to her and put an arm around her shoulders. "I think it must be my fault," she said. "The crystal is mine. Some kind of energy I was emitting made the alp focus on you."

"You mean, like, you were mad at me?" Val asked.

Ronnie's cheeks reddened. "A little," she admitted, "at first. Well, for a few years now."

"What?" Val said. "Years?!"

"I was jealous," Ronnie said.

Val couldn't believe her ears. "You?" Val said. "The cool girl in the city with trips all over the world and a fancy car and apartment? You were jealous of *me*?"

"Of course," Ronnie said. "Your parents are always around, always doing things with you, so interested in your life."

"Aren't yours?" Val asked.

"Ha," Ronnie said. "Dad's hardly said a word to me in five years, and Mum almost never pulls her eyes from her precious huge TV in their bedroom.

"Besides," she went on, "your parents didn't pick you up from the town and school and *friends* you loved to move to a big, scary city."

"I suppose I never thought of it that way," Val said. "Sorry."

Ronnie shrugged one shoulder. "I'm over it," she said. "Especially after last night."

The girls sat quietly.

"It's late," Ronnie said.

"We should get ready," Val said.

Ronnie took the book, closed it, and put it on the carpet. Then she placed the yellow crystal on top of it. "Do you have the hammer?" she asked.

Val jumped up, opened her desk drawer, and pulled out her dad's biggest, baddest-looking hammer. She'd "borrowed" it while their parents had been chatting after supper. "Will this do?" she asked.

"Oh, yeah," Ronnie said. There was that wicked grin. It didn't seem quite so wicked at the moment. "That'll definitely do."

* * *

For an hour, the girls sat face to face on the carpet, the book and crystal between them. Val held the hammer in her lap, fidgeting with it as the minutes ticked by.

There came a knock at the door. The girls jumped.

"Lights out please, girls," Dad said.

"OK!" Val said, and she jumped up to turn off the overhead light.

Ronnie waited a moment and clicked on the bedside lamp, which the girls had placed on the floor beside the book.

"I don't think I'm ready," Val said.

"Sure you are," Ronnie said. "Remember: you just have to smash the crystal *while* the alp is watching you. If it doesn't see, it doesn't work. We'll be stuck with it forever."

Forever, Val thought. That meant she'd only have one chance to get it right. If the beast looked away as she smashed the crystal, there would be no second chance.

Val shook her head and handed Ronnie the hammer. "You do it," Val said. "I'll mess it up."

Ronnie took the hammer, and at the same moment, the bulb in the lamp blew with a pop. Thick smoke and an acrid smell filled the air.

Val coughed as she fumbled for the overhead light switch. "Where is it?" she muttered. Finally her hand found the switch.

The overhead light flickered and crackled. Yellow smoke hovered through the room. Ronnie stood beside Val, and the girls turned slowly in the flickering dim light, barely able to see.

"I'm getting my dad," Val said, reaching for the doorknob. She tugged the door and found it locked. "Not again . . ."

The girls pressed their backs to the door and huddled close together. Ronnie held the hammer in both fists. Her hands shook, and the hammer trembled.

The light flickered once, twice, three

times, and then the room fell into total darkness. The girls shrieked, and the beast appeared.

It crouched on the headboard of Val's bed, its eyes brighter than ever. Its terrifying claws dug into the wood of the headboard. Its grin shone in the dim light, as yellow as that crystal.

The crystal. It sat in the centre of the room, glowing as brightly now as a full moon.

"It's watching us!" Val said. "Do it now!"

Ronnie seemed to snap out of a trance and remembered she was holding the hammer. She dived into the middle of the room and raised the hammer, but as she did, the alp leaped from the headboard with a wild roar.

Ronnie screamed and dropped the hammer. Val grabbed Ronnie's hand and pulled her away from the beast. They cowered against the wardrobe door.

"I will devour you both," the alp snarled.

The monster's voice sounded surprisingly human. "Both my caller and my victim. I am never sated."

The alp leaped across the room, lithe and graceful, and reached them in one bound. The girls dived apart, Val to take cover under her desk, and Ronnie crouched under the window. The alp growled and followed Ronnie.

Ronnie shrieked and knocked the bedside table over to block the monster.

Val took the opportunity to crawl out from under the desk and snatch up the crystal from the middle of the rug. It glowed brighter as she held it, but the hammer was nowhere to be found.

She searched the carpet and even under the bed using the evil crystal as a torch, but it was no use. Meanwhile, Ronnie held a table lamp like a weapon, swinging it wildly at the alp to keep him at bay.

"Smash it, Val!" Ronnie shrieked. "Hurry!"

Ronnie smashed the lamp against the alp's face. For a moment, he stood confused, blinking and snarling. She scurried past him and took cover under the bed.

Val looked desperately around her for anything heavy. Next to the door she found something: Ronnie's chunky boots. Val grabbed one, went to her desk, and put down the glowing crystal.

"Hey, ugly!" Val shouted.

The creature snarled and faced her.

"Look at this!" Val lifted the boot and brought down the heel as hard as she could on the crystal.

The crystal shattered to dust, sending another acrid yellow cloud in a poof into Val's face. The alp cried out as if in pain as the air in the room swirled around it like a miniature tornado.

It picked up the monster, and it shrunk inside the swirling dust until it vanished completely. The tornado weakened, and soon the room was still and quiet – though a bit messier than it had been a few minutes before.

Val coughed and stumbled to Ronnie's side, where she lay next to the bedside table.

"Are you . . . OK?" Val asked, lying beside her.

Ronnie coughed into her fist and nodded. "I think so," she said.

"Is it over?" Val said.

"The alp is gone," Ronnie said. "That's good enough for me."

"Me too," Val said.

Val felt Ronnie's hand wrap around her own, and she turned to look at her. Her cousin's short hair was messy, stuck to her forehead with sweat and a smudge of drying blood beneath a scratch above her eye.

"You did it," Ronnie said.

"I know," Val said, barely able to believe it herself.

"Your face is covered in that stuff," Ronnie said. She sat up and grabbed her towel, hanging on the back of Val's desk chair. "That yellow dust."

"Thanks," Val said, wiping her face.

As the smoke cleared, and the girls' heart rates slowed to normal, they sat up. Val picked up the book from the middle of the floor and sat on the edge of the bed.

Ronnie sat beside her.

The door flung open.

"What was all that racket in here?" Dad snapped.

Behind him, Mum, Aunt Jackie and Uncle Anton gathered in their dressing gowns and gawked into the room.

"Racket?" Ronnie said. "We're just reading."

"Yep," Val said. "You know, silly stuff. Fantasy stories."

CHAPTER FOURTEEN

"I wish you could stay another week," Val said. She held Ronnie against her in a long farewell hug.

"Me too," Ronnie said. "But now that we aren't jealous of each other anymore, hopefully we'll visit more often."

"Definitely," Val said. "I can't believe I'm saying this, but I actually had fun."

"Even though we were almost devoured by a monster?" Ronnie said as she pulled away from the hug.

Val nodded.

"And even though you don't even believe in magic anymore?" Ronnie asked. Her mouth curved into that distinct, crooked smile.

"I suppose I do," Val admitted, "a little."

"I know," Ronnie said. "You always have. That's why I left the book on your bed."

Val actually bounced on her toes and clapped. "I can't wait to read it," she said. "But I didn't give you anything."

"Sure you did," Ronnie said. She pulled a book out of the side pocket of her duffel: Val's diary.

"Hey!" Val said. She grabbed it and hugged it to her chest.

"I told you I liked your poems," Ronnie said. "I want to read the rest."

Val sighed and half smiled. "Fine," she said, handing the diary back to her cousin. "Keep it."

"Yeah?" Ronnie said. "Thanks." She flipped through the pages before slipping it back into her duffel.

Val shrugged. "It's nearly full anyway," she said. "Besides, I think it's time to start a new one."

"More poems?" Ronnie asked.

Val shook her head. "Time to move on from poems," she said.

Ronnie's eyes went wide. "But they're so good," she said.

"Thanks," Val said. "But I'm going to focus on my first true love: fantasy stories."

Ronnie nodded slowly. "Good plan," she said. "I can't wait to read what you dream up."

Val shook her head vigorously. "Nope," she said. "No more dreams, thank you very much."

Ronnie laughed. Uncle Anton honked the

car horn. Aunt Jackie stuck her head out the passenger-side window.

"Come on, Veronica!" she called.

"I'd better go," Ronnie said.

The cousins had another quick hug goodbye. Ronnie darted to the car and climbed into the back seat.

"Hey, Val," she said, sticking her head out the window. "We're going to Romania in October. Want me to bring you back something?"

Val shook her head. "Sure," Val said. "How about something safe, like a snowglobe?"

"Aw," Ronnie said. "I was thinking maybe a vampire. Or a werewolf!"

With that, Uncle Anton pulled off the driveway and took off down the road. Val waved madly as the car disappeared around the corner.

CHAPTER FIFTEEN

That night as Val got ready for bed, her room seemed a little empty without Ronnie's sleeping bag on the floor. Without *Ronnie*.

She found Ronnie's book of the occult on her bed and sat down with the book on her lap. To her surprise, it fell open on its own to a page towards the back.

The page was littered with tiny handwriting and a handful of drawings in ink. In ornate letters across the top of the page it read: "How to safely dispose of your shattered Alp crystal's dust."

Val's heart stopped as she scanned the room for the dust of the broken crystal. She jumped up and ran to her desk, her heart now pounding at double speed.

The dust of the crystal was still there, and Val gasped. It was no longer merely a pile of grayed yellow dust.

As if someone had spent hours at work on the dust, it now formed a distinct shape: a complex pattern, with swirls and angles and fine lines. A rune of some kind, maybe.

Without thinking, she wiped the symbol away. The dust fell to the rug. Some stuck to her hand, like a thousand tiny splinters of glass. Val ran to the book to read the instructions on the open page, but they were gone. *The instructions were gone.*

All that remained on the page was an ink drawing, scratchy-looking, as if the artist had been in a hurry to complete it. It was the alp again, but now its face stretched in an agonized howl.

Its teeth were longer, sharper and stained black. Two spiralling horns jutted from its forehead. Its dark hair was matted with mud, as if it had crawled up from the depths of the earth.

It stared off the page, right at Val.

Across the top of the page, the ornate lettering was gone. In its place, in scratchy letters, ragged and sloppy as if carved with a claw, were the words: "You did it wrong. It will be back."

GLOSSARY

acrid strong, unpleasant

aghast shocked and dismayed

coven meeting or band of witches

cynical having a scornful attitude towards ideas

dormer part of a house that sticks out from a sloping roof. A window is set into the dormer.

dryads nymphs living in the woods

fantasize indulge in fantasy or daydreams

feign pretend to be affected by something

hierarchy person or things arranged in ranks or classes

idly not busy or not working

occult relating to supernatural forces

Ouija board board marked with letters of the alphabet and other signs, used in seances to receive messages said to come from people who are dead

pentagram flat shape of a star with five points, formed by five straight lines

planchette small platform on which fingertips rest, their slight pressure causing the platform to move and spell out words

rune mysterious symbol believed to have magical properties

sated fully satisfied

seance meeting at which people try to make contact with and talk to the spirits of dead people

sinewy strong and lean

undeterred continuing something despite setbacks

DISCUSSION QUESTIONS

1. Val and Ronnie imagined themselves in fantasy worlds when they were younger. Discuss how Val and Ronnie's interests changed as they grew older.

2. How was the alp in this story different from other elves you've read about? Discuss which stories you've read that had elves in them and how they compared to the elves in this story.

3. Val sees glowing lights that look like eyes in the dark. Have you ever seen something in the dark that looked scary? Discuss how you reacted to it. Did it turn out to be something different from what you expected?

WRITING PROMPTS

1. Val keeps a diary to write about her life and to write poems. Write a diary entry from her perspective the night after she and Ronnie defeat the alp.

2. Do you have any relatives or friends like Ronnie? Write a few sentences about the differences and similarities between them and Ronnie, using examples of Ronnie from the text.

3. The alp leaves a message that it's not finished with Val and Ronnie. Write what you think happens after the story ends.

ABOUT THE AUTHOR

Eric Stevens lives in St. Paul, Minnesota, USA. He is studying to become a middle-school English teacher. Some of his favourite things include pizza, playing video games, watching cooking programmes on TV, riding his bike and trying out new restaurants. Some of his least favourite things include olives and shovelling snow.

ABOUT THE ILLUSTRATOR

Neil Evans lives on the south coast of the UK with his partner and their imaginary cat. Evans is a comic artist, illustrator and general all-around doodler of whatever nonsense pops into his head. He contributes regularly to the British underground comics scene, and he is currently writing and illustrating a number of graphic novels and picture book hybrids for older children.

FAIRY TALE OR HORROR STORY?

When we hear the word *elf*, we may think of an immortal archer, a fairy or just a powerful enchanter. Usually, we see elves as good creatures in popular culture. So why is the alp in this story a monster? The reason is that elves have changed over the centuries. All of the stories today of alps, fairies and even Legolas from *The Hobbit* come from ancient European folk tales.

Originally the elf was a powerful, supernatural creature who daily caused problems that couldn't be explained. Roaming Germanic tribes told stories about elves in oral tradition, then settled in modern Britain, Germany and Scandinavia and brought elf stories with them. Then, as languages evolved into modern German,

English, French and others, many of these stories became fairy tales that we know today.

In some older tales, an elf's hex could cause food to spoil early. "Elf-shot", an elf's invisible arrow, created sudden pains and illness in people and animals. Children enchanted by an elf's magic would lose their sense of direction in the forest. In other stories, however, showing kindness to a stranger may reveal the stranger to be a disguised elf! Instead of harming anyone, the elf uses its powers to return the good deed. Still, as magical creatures and shapeshifters, everyone knew elves could not be trusted.

In Germany, these tales created a version of the elf called the *alp*, a vampiric monster that stalked and enchanted people while they slept. Meanwhile, all around Europe, the *elf* became a mischievous little character that might fix a cobbler's shoes, work for Santa Claus or play harmless tricks on people.

What about the elves in your favourite films, games and books? In the past and today, writers have looked at old tales and myths to inspire new stories. William Shakespeare's *A Midsummer Night's Dream* is a good example that turned elves from fairy tale creatures into characters in one of the most popular plays of all time. Like Shakespeare, modern writers want to turn older tales into fresh ideas for their stories, much like the alp in this story or the elves of *The Lord of the Rings*. By looking at the folktales of Germany, a modern horror story was created; perhaps one day we will be reading an elf story that is even more surprising!

SPINE SHIVERS